SONIC THE HEDGEHOG

SONIC AND THE TALES OF DECEPTION

PENGUIN YOUNG READERS LICENSES
An Imprint of Penguin Random House LLC

Copyright © 2018 by SEGA®. All rights reserved. Published by
Penguin Young Readers Licenses, an imprint of Penguin Random House LLC,
345 Hudson Street, New York, New York 10014.
Manufactured in China.

ISBN 9781524784744
10 9 8 7 6 5 4 3 2 1

SONIC AND THE TALES OF DECEPTION

by Jake Black

illustrated by Ian McGinty

with Alo Covarrubias, Tabby Freeman, Axur Eneas

Penguin Young Readers Licenses
An Imprint of Penguin Random House

Not-So-Fantastic JOURNEY

WHAM! Another robot slammed into the wall, breaking into two, now inanimate, pieces of junk metal. Sonic turned around to see that it was Knuckles who had stopped the robot right before it had reached him. He gave him a quick nod as they both kept fighting and shouted, "Thanks. That was a close one!"

The day began like any other day. Sonic, Tails, Knuckles, and Amy Rose learned that a small army of Dr. Eggman's robots had descended on the city and were wreaking havoc everywhere. As usual, the team raced to the scene and leaped into action. Sonic sped up and down buildings, leaping off them, smashing through the outer shells of robot after robot. Tails weaved his plane in and around the cityscape, blasting robots into oblivion. Knuckles and Amy Rose used their strength and fighting skills to dominate several other

robots. It almost seemed too easy. And perhaps it was.

Not far from the scene of the battle, Dr. Eggman observed the fight between his creations and Team Sonic from a floating platform. Smiling, he pulled a small remote control from his pocket. He pressed a small button on the side of the remote.

Suddenly, from beneath the platform, a swarm of what appeared to be bees formed a cloud around Eggman.

"Finally! My ultimate plan has come to pass! These robot bee stings will inject Sonic with tiny nanobots that will take over his cellular structure and turn him into a robot—a robot that I can control!" Eggman said and laughed. "Fly, my pretties!"

The swarm drifted high into the air and began the flight toward Sonic and his friends in the city.

Unaware of the oncoming cloud of robot bees, Sonic stood with his friends in the middle of the carnage, and smashed and shattered the remains of the evil robots surrounding them.

"Nothing like totally winning another fight with Eggman's loser 'bots!" Sonic said, his friends laughing.

"Oh, Sonic," Amy Rose giggled, "you were amazing, as always."

Tails and Knuckles rolled their eyes at each other.

"You're right, I was!" Sonic said.

"Whatever," Knuckles said. "You couldn't've done it without us."

"Could so!" Sonic replied, pretending to be offended by his friend's words.

"What I don't totally understand, is why it was so easy to beat these robots. Something's up," Tails said, sounding unusually worried.

"Easy?! There were like a million robots. That wasn't easy!" Knuckles protested.

"No, he's right," Sonic said. "It's almost like it was supposed to be a distraction. Eggman's up to some—" Tails raised his hand. "Shhh. What's that noise?" he asked.

The group went silent. In the distance, they heard a humming noise. It grew louder and louder. The sky darkened as the cloud of bees shrouded the sun.

"What . . . what is that?" Amy Rose asked, her voice quivering.

"Eggman's distraction," Sonic said. The cloud of robot bees shrunk and morphed into an almost-solid cube. The cube picked up speed as it hurled toward Sonic. The speedy hedgehog was poised to strike. Just as he was about to run toward the cube, the cube exploded into a spherical swarm. Each of the thousands of robot bees pointed their stingers toward Sonic and were moving down on top of him in sphere formation. Sonic's eyes grew wide. He'd never seen anything like it before. Paralyzed in wonder, Sonic could only stare as the bees moved faster and closer to him.

"Sonic! Move!" Tails yelled. But it was no use, Sonic was hypnotized by the bees.

Knuckles jumped into action. The red echidna climbed rapidly up the wall of a nearby building and sprang off toward Sonic. The bees were getting close, only inches from Sonic.

Knuckles collided with Sonic, slamming the hedgehog to the ground and out of the bees' path, snapping him out of his hypnotic trance. Sonic stood just in time to see the sphere of bees cover Knuckles, stinging him all over his body.

Seconds later, the bees regrouped as the cube and flew away, high into the sky. Sonic, Tails, and Amy Rose stood over Knuckles.

"Uggghhhh . . . what . . . happened?" Knuckles managed to say as he moaned. "I . . . I don't . . . I don't feel right."

"We've got to get him back to my lab," Tails said urgently.

⟩⟩⟩⟩⟩⟩⟩⟩

Back in Tails' lab, Knuckles was flat on his back and connected to several different machines. The brilliant fox was examining a strange spot on Knuckles' arm.

"Guys, come check this out," Tails said. Sonic and Amy Rose joined him, peering at the weird metallic spot that was slowly growing on Knuckles' arm.

"I think those bees are turning Knuckles into a robot," Tails said matter-of-factly.

"How is that possible?" Amy Rose asked.

Sonic turned away, angrily. "Eggman. He has to be behind this. Those robots we beat *were* a distraction, like we thought—a distraction so those bees could sting me and turn me into a robot."

"Exactly," Tails said. "I think those bees' stingers injected Knuckles with microscopic robots—nanobots—that are rewriting his body and turning him into a robot."

Amy Rose teared up. "Is there anything we can do?"

"We have one shot, but it's a long one," Tails said. "We have to get inside Knuckles and destroy the nanobots that have started to take over his body."

"Inside?" Amy Rose asked, confused.

"Yes," Tails replied, walking across the lab to a large machine topped by a laser. "We can use the Super Shrink Ray and enter his body through that robotic spot on his arm."

"I'm going in," Sonic said.

"I thought you might say that," Tails said. "Here's what I think: It looks like the nanobots are just like any other beehive. They have a 'queen' that's controlling them. Plus, I think they're self-replicating or something . . . anyways, they have orders from the queen to complete their task, so they will not stop until they do."

"Or until I defeat the queen," Sonic said.

"Exactly," said Tails.

"Knock out the hive. Got it. Where's the queen gonna be so I can kick her tail?" Sonic asked.

"I don't know exactly, but I bet she's inside Knuckles' brain," Tails said.

Sonic nodded. "Let's do this," he said.

>>>>>>>>

Deep inside his hideout, Dr. Eggman welcomed his swarm of bees back into their mechanical hive. Like real honeybees, with the loss of their stingers, the robots would soon shut down forever. Eggman, disappointed the bees were unable to get to Sonic, took comfort in knowing that Sonic would suffer from watching his friend disappear.

He pressed a button on the remote control to turn on the nanobots' cameras and then turned on a computer monitor to watch. The nanobots inside of Knuckles' body were busy replacing his biological parts with robotic parts. "This won't take long at all," Eggman said, and then laughed.

〉〉〉〉〉〉〉〉

Sonic stood in front of the Shrink Ray. He was angry: angry that Eggman had attacked; angry that Knuckles got hurt; angry that he was so hypnotized by the bees in the first place. But, even as angry as he was, he was excited to fight the nanobots inside Knuckles. This was an adventure and a rescue mission all in one. And one that required him to go fast, before it was too late. And Sonic loved going fast.

Tails gave Sonic a handheld digital map of Knuckles' innards. A flashing dot showed Sonic his location on the map. He'd be able to use it to find his way around the maze of Knuckles' organs.

"This might tickle," Tails said as he flipped the switch on the Shrink Ray.

A blast of green-white light burst out of the machine, and an instant later, Sonic disappeared from sight, shrunken to an almost-microscopic level. Tails used a pair of tweezers to pick Sonic up from the ground. He and Amy Rose were careful not to speak as the sound waves from their voices could have moved Sonic like he was blown by a massive hurricane. Carefully, Tails set Sonic into the metal spot on Knuckles' arm. It looked to Sonic like the doorway into a massive steel castle. He stepped inside and found a metallic hallway that led to an opening of muscle tissue.

Sonic ran to the muscle tissue and looked around the inside of Knuckles' arm. He was amazed by what he saw. The nanobots were all moving rapidly throughout the arm, replacing nerves, muscles, ligaments, and other tissues with robot parts. It was almost like the nanobots were overwriting these tissues with their technological organs.

"This place is crazy!" Sonic said, pushing a button on the map device. "How do I get to Knuckles' brain?"

"Follow the nerves in Knuckles' arm to get to his brain," the computerized voice of the map device said.

Sonic looked around the city of body tissues until he spotted what looked to be power lines running throughout. There were small electrical sparks crackling along the power lines. Nerves. Sonic began to run alongside the nerves. He picked up speed, racing toward the brain—where all the nerves would come together.

Suddenly, a pair of nanobots cut him off as he ran. Sonic curled himself into a ball to avoid smashing into the nanobots. Rolling to a stop directly in front of the robotic bacteria, Sonic watched as the nanobots began planting their technological body parts over the nerve Sonic was following.

"Knock it off, you guys. You're getting on my nerves!" Sonic said. "Er . . . actually, Knuckles' nerves, I guess. Whatever. Just stop."

The nanobots turned for a brief second to glance at Sonic and returned to their work. Sonic smirked.

"That's how you want to play it, fine; that's how we'll play it," Sonic said.

Sonic ran toward the nanobots and threw a mighty punch at the one closest to him. The nanobot shattered into a million pieces. The second nanobot continued to work on the nerve. Surprised and emboldened at how easily the first nanobot was destroyed, Sonic wound up and blasted the second nanobot with a massive punch. It shattered just as easily as the first.

Sonic laughed. *Whoa! This isn't gonna be hard at all! These things are totally wimpy!* he thought to himself.

No sooner had he finished that thought than another pair of nanobots arrived and began working on the nerve exactly where the first two had been. Sonic destroyed those, and they were immediately replaced by another set. He was going to need to get to the queen.

Sonic jumped back into running along the muscle tissue. Because Knuckles was strong, his muscles were firm and tight—it was actually the perfect type of stuff to be running on. With the power-line-like nerve crackling above him, Sonic ran as fast as he could, heading up to Knuckles' brain.

>>>>>>>>

Dr. Eggman had stepped away from his monitors for only a minute—even mad scientists have to eat once in a while—but when he returned, he heard the computers blaring an alarm.

"Warning. Intruder. Damage to nanobots. Warning. Intruder. Damage to nanobots," the computer repeated.

Dr. Eggman hurriedly sat down and examined the monitors. He could see the nanobots Sonic had destroyed. He pressed some buttons to change to different cameras. And then he saw it. The blue blur he hated more than anything in the world.

"Sonic," Dr. Eggman hissed.

Typing quickly into his computer, Eggman ordered the nanobots to attack Sonic. Dozens of nanobots inside

Knuckles' body left their tasks of robotizing and moved in a mini-swarm to Sonic's location near Knuckles' shoulder.

"Maybe I'll get the Sonic I want after all," Eggman said, pleased.

》》》》》》》

Sonic had been running and dodging obstacles—both biological and technological—throughout Knuckles' body. He was nearing the collarbone and neck. Just a little farther and Sonic would be in Knuckles' head on his way to the brain. But that would have to wait another minute.

Sonic screeched to a halt, sliding on Knuckles' collarbone. Eggman's mini-swarm of assault nanobots gathered around him. They looked a lot like the swarm of bees that had distracted Sonic earlier, but he wasn't going to let them hypnotize him this time.

The nanobots encroached, and Sonic blasted them away. He ran in a circle, creating a whirlwind that yanked several nanobots from the swarm and smashed them against each other in the funnel of wind. He rolled himself into a ball and bowled over another group of the nanobots, sending nanobot shrapnel flying everywhere. He spun in the air, kicking through countless more. In a few short moments, the attacking nanobots had all been destroyed.

"I'm not gonna wait around for replacements to show up!" Sonic said and hurled himself back into action.

Sonic arrived at the base of Knuckles' neck. The nervous system turned upward, but there wasn't much he could run on to follow it to the brain. Sonic noticed Knuckles' windpipe was right in front of him. If he could catch the wind current when Knuckles breathed out, he could ride that up into Knuckles' head.

Watching the movement in Knuckles' neck in order to time his leap, Sonic stepped backward to give himself room to run. At the right moment, Sonic sped forward and jumped into the middle of Knuckles' throat. For a brief second, Sonic panicked that he'd mistimed his jump and Knuckles was breathing in, the air pushing Sonic downward. But before he could even finish that thought, Sonic felt his body soaring upward on a stream of air carrying him into Knuckles' head.

Sonic moved toward the back of Knuckles' head—near the base of his skull. He followed the hundreds of nerves that had converged at Knuckles' spine, and climbed up into his friend's brain.

"I'm actually in Knuckles' brain. That's so weird," Sonic whispered to himself.

Sonic could see a cluster of nanobots that surrounded a larger nanobot—the queen. There was no time for hesitation. Sonic zoomed from the base of the brain straight to the queen and her minions. He moved so quickly that the minion nanobots didn't put up any sort of fight. He'd caught them off guard. Leaping from the carnage of the shattered minions, Sonic landed atop the queen nanobot. With superspeed, Sonic curled his body into a ball and charged toward the queen nanobot in a mighty spin attack, blasting the queen into oblivion. The queen destroyed, Sonic looked around in awe as the carcasses of the other nanobots disappeared. By destroying the queen, Sonic had caused all the bees to self-destruct. The plan worked! Knuckles was free of the nanobots.

"Mission accomplished, Tails . . . as if there were any doubt!" Sonic whispered to himself as he glanced at the map of Knuckles' insides.

"How do I get out of here?" Sonic asked the map.

The map told him to go back down near the windpipe and take a left at Knuckles' nose.

"His nose? Gross!" Sonic said.

Eggman roared in anger. By destroying the queen, Sonic had destroyed all the nanobots and bees Eggman had ever created.

"Next time, Sonic. Next time," Eggman promised.

A few hours later, after Sonic had climbed out of Knuckles' nose and Tails had unshrunk him, the team gathered around Knuckles who was still on Tails' lab table.

"How are you feeling, Knuckles?" Amy Rose asked.

"Ugh," was pretty much all Knuckles could say.

"Thanks for taking the hit for me," Sonic said. "I mean, I probably would have stopped them at the last minute, but still . . ."

Tails rolled his eyes. Knuckles looked at Sonic. "You'd have done the same for me. But next time you have to shrink down and go inside my body, don't climb on my spine. I still feel your footprints back there!"

"Deal!" Sonic laughed.

FIGHTING SHADOW

Sonic didn't like to sleep. At all. But tonight he was more tired than usual. He couldn't explain it, but he simply could not stay awake. He dreamed of destroying Dr. Eggman's robots and defeating the deranged scientist once and for all. It was a good dream.

Miles away, though, the real Dr. Eggman was about to unleash a new, sinister plan. He had invented a long-range mind-control device and was going to direct it at Sonic. Standing at the device's controls, Dr. Eggman turned some knobs and rotated some dials, finishing some final tests. It was ready. It looked like a small

speaker, and was directed out the window of Dr. Eggman's lab, toward Sonic's home.

"I've completed the first phase of the plan: blasting sound waves that made Sonic unable to stay awake," Dr. Eggman said, laughing creepily and spinning another dial.

"And now I've developed the proper frequency that only Sonic can hear, which will allow me to take over his mind and place him under my control!"

Dr. Eggman pressed a couple of buttons and tapped on a touch screen, verifying the frequency setting of the device. Tiny sound waves shot out of a very advanced-looking speaker, vibrated for miles through the air, and somehow headed directly toward sleeping Sonic.

In his bed, Sonic snored slightly, muttering something about victory over Dr. Eggman. The sound waves from Eggman's machine moved through the window and penetrated Sonic's ear. They vibrated with a piercing frequency that forced Sonic to wake with a jump.

"What's that noise?" he shrieked, covering his ears. But it was too late. The sound waves had connected with his brain. He heard a voice in his head. "Sonic . . ."

"Dr. Eggman?" Sonic asked, recognizing the voice as his archenemy's.

"Sonic . . . You are now under my control . . ." Eggman's voice echoed in Sonic's head.

Sonic was trying to fight off the voice and its powerful suggestions, but he couldn't. Within seconds, the pain subsided and he relaxed his will—completely under Dr. Eggman's influence.

"Yes, master," Sonic said weakly.

"Sonic. Come to my lair. It's time to begin your training," Eggman ordered.

Sonic raced out of his home, running at top speed toward Dr. Eggman's evil laboratory.

>>>>>>>>

Seconds later, he arrived. Dr. Eggman was waiting for him on the grass outside his hideout. Dr. Eggman motioned for Sonic to follow him inside. Sonic's lips curled into an evil grin. He was ready to learn the ways of world domination from his new master.

Inside the lair, Sonic saw hundreds, maybe even thousands, of robots. They were all different and served different purposes. He began to realize these were Dr. Eggman's soldiers who would carry out the mad scientist's nefarious plans. And he was expecting Sonic to act as their general, leading them into war against the world, until the entire planet was ruled by Dr. Eggman.

As Sonic saw the robots, he felt a sense of anger toward them. He was having flashes of memories of him fighting Eggman and these robots, but the memories felt wrong,

like he'd joined the wrong side all along. He was happy Dr. Eggman had set him free from his good ways of the past.

"Sonic, your first attack will be on the beachfront, just outside of the city. I want you to take twenty robots and destroy all the buildings along the boardwalk. This won't take over the world, but it will send a message to everyone that they better get out of our way!" Eggman said.

Sonic sneered confidently. This wouldn't be a problem. In fact, he thought, it would be fun.

〉〉〉〉〉〉〉〉

Hours later, Knuckles and Amy Rose burst into Tails' lab.

"The beachfront is under attack by Eggman's robots!" Amy Rose said with a high level of concern in her voice.

"And we can't find Sonic," Knuckles said gruffly.

The team nodded at each other. They knew what they had to do. They raced to Tails' plane and soared toward the beach.

From the air, they could see the chaos of the robots smashing buildings and people running from the beach toward safety. The robots were terrorizing countless innocents and destroying everything in their path.

Tails swooped his plane downward, weaving around the robots and blasting them with laser cannons. Amy Rose and Knuckles leaped from the plane and began manually battling the robots in hand-to-hand combat.

As Knuckles threw punch after punch at robot after robot, he saw a familiar blue blur from the corner of his eye.

"You guys! Sonic's here!" Knuckles cheered. But the team's relief and celebrations would be brief. No sooner had Knuckles declared Sonic's presence than the blue hedgehog attacked his friends. Running at full speed, Sonic jumped into the air, landing on the nose of Tails' plane. Sonic grabbed the controls from Tails and forced the plane into a nosedive.

"Sonic! No!" Amy Rose screamed. For a moment, Sonic seemed to break from his trance and released the controls.

Sonic jumped off the plane and ran away, leading the handful of robots his friends hadn't destroyed in the retreat to safety.

Tails pulled the nose of his plane upward enough at the last minute to land the plane safely. Knuckles and Amy Rose approached the plane.

"What just happened?" Amy Rose asked, tears filling her eyes.

Knuckles punched the plane and growled in frustration. "Sonic's betrayed all of us!" he said.

Tails stared off into the distance where Sonic and the robots had gone. He'd never seen Sonic like this. Something was very wrong.

"When he jumped on the plane, I looked into his eyes. It's like he was Sonic, but wasn't Sonic at the same time. He was . . . different . . . ," Tails said.

"Yeah, evil," Knuckles said, unable to hide his bitterness.

"What are we going to do? There has to be some way we can help him. Some way we can get the old Sonic back!" Amy Rose pleaded.

Tails rubed his chin as he thought.

"I have an idea," Tails said. "If we're going to save 'Evil Sonic' and make him good again, we need to understand how he's thinking. And there is only one person in the world who can teach us . . ."

〉〉〉〉〉〉〉〉

Shadow the Hedgehog was alone in his home, lost in his own thoughts. He was so deep in thought, Shadow was almost oblivious to Tails and Knuckles approaching him.

"Shadow . . . ," Tails said.

"What?" Shadow replied coldly.

"We need your help. We think Sonic's been captured and turned evil by Dr. Eggman."

Shadow didn't care—at all. And he made that clear to

Tails. "So? How does that affect me?"

"I guess it doesn't, really. But we were hoping you'd help us figure out a way to get Sonic back from the dark side," Tails said.

"Not interested," Shadow replied.

Knuckles moved past Tails. "Listen, buster. Sonic is evil. You're kind of like Evil Sonic. You understand what he's thinking. If you don't help us figure it out and stop him, Sonic and Eggman are going to take over the world. And do you really want Sonic to be the one who helps Eggman rule the planet?"

Shadow wasn't evil, but he didn't like being compared to Sonic in any way. That made him mad—really mad. However, deep down, Shadow respected Sonic, and if Eggman had turned Sonic evil, that had to be corrected.

"All right. Fine. I'll help," Shadow said.

〉〉〉〉〉〉〉〉

Shadow showed up in Tails' lab only a few moments later.

"So, what's the plan?" Shadow asked. Amy Rose and Knuckles looked blankly at each other.

"I thought you were going to tell us," Amy Rose said.

Shadow rolled his eyes, "I'm only here to tell you what's in Sonic's head. I'm not going to make your battle plans."

Knuckles stood up and moved uncomfortably close to Shadow. "Your intel is going to make the plan. We're going to rescue him, and you're going to tell us how. Got it?"

Shadow pushed past Knuckles, ignoring the warning. He walked toward one of Tails' computers.

"So, genius-fox, how did Eggman turn Sonic toward the dark side in the first place?" Shadow asked.

"Well, I checked out Sonic's bedroom and found nothing out of place; there were no signs of a struggle," Tails said. "So

35

how does one get inside of a person's head to turn him evil without a fight?" he asked them.

They all glanced around with blank looks on their faces.

Tails sighed. "I think Eggman may have used some kind of sound-wave device that vibrated at a frequency only Sonic could hear," he said. "Those sound waves could have easily carried subliminal messages into Sonic's brain, basically re-wiring him."

"So, like a 'hedgehog whistle'?" Shadow said. "You want to know what's in his head? Whatever Eggman's telling him. And based on the attack on the beachfront, it looks like he's telling him to burn the world down."

"I have an invention that will blast sound waves of the opposite frequency at Sonic. Using the principle of destructive interference, it should cancel out Eggman's 'Sonic whistle,'" Tails said, holding up a small box roughly the size of a cell phone. "The problem is, it's got a very limited range. It basically has to be within a couple of inches of Sonic. And you're the only person I know who might be able to run fast enough to get close enough to him."

This caught Shadow's attention. "Might be?" he asked.

"Well, yeah. He's pretty fast. Faster than you, I think," Tails said.

In less than a blink of an eye, Shadow zipped around Tails, snatching the sound device from his hand.

"Not. Faster. Than. Me," Shadow said defiantly.

Suddenly an alarm sounded in Tails' lab, echoing throughout his house. Another attack was underway. This time in the heart of the city. Sonic was leading dozens of robots, and there was no one standing in their way.

Shadow said nothing, but sped away to the battlefront in a black blur.

Knuckles leaned into Tails. "Why didn't you tell us about your little destructive interference invention in the first place?"

"Do you really think Shadow would've come all this way just for that?" Tails smiled.

"Probably not," Knuckles said.

"Probably not," Tails agreed.

》》》》》》》

Sonic could still hear the piercing sound that Eggman was using to control him, but he didn't care. It no longer hurt or bothered him. As long as he could take over the world, that was enough. And it was beginning in the city. Sonic led the robots into the middle of the city, and they were driving the citizens and residents into the streets. It was chaotic.

But chaos wouldn't bother Shadow, who sped into town from the city's other end. He was carrying the disruptive interference device and was poised to use it on Sonic as soon as he got close.

"Hey! Sonic! Think you can outrun me?" Shadow said.

Sonic shot Shadow a passing glance but paid him little heed. Shadow raced toward Sonic, but Sonic dashed out of the way, weaving his way through the destructive robots. Shadow was trying to navigate the obstacle course of the battle, but was finding it hard as the robots kept interfering.

Shadow shoved one robot out of the way as he ran past; another he used as a springboard, leaping into the air to try to make up ground.

Just as he was about to reach Sonic, Shadow felt something hard hit his ankle. One of the robots tripped Shadow. The interference device flew from Shadow's hand into the rubble and chaos in the city streets.

He couldn't even see it.

"Great," Shadow whispered to himself.

Shadow searched through the rubble. He couldn't find the device anywhere. Without it, he knew it would be almost impossible to defeat Sonic. Or free him from Eggman's control. And then Sonic would be in charge. Not. Cool.

〉〉〉〉〉〉〉〉

Overhead, Shadow saw Tails' plane joining the fight. Amy Rose and Knuckles were battling robots on the ground. Shadow grew more frantic, searching for the interference device.

"Looking for this?"

Shadow spun around to see Sonic standing on a pile of rubble, holding the interference device.

"Give it back!" Shadow said through gritted teeth.

Sonic examined the box in his hands. "What is it? A weapon?"

Shadow glared at Sonic, determined to get the device back. "Something like that. It's a device that makes me even faster than you . . . not that I need it."

"Well, let's give it a try," Sonic said as he pushed a

flashing button on the device. Suddenly, the interference sound waves blasted from the box through Sonic's ears and into his brain. The sound waves clashed with the sound waves coming from Eggman's machine that was controlling Sonic. Within seconds, both waves had canceled each other out.

Sonic fell to the ground, holding his head. Shadow took a step toward Sonic.

"You okay, Sonic?" Shadow asked.

Sonic looked up, angry. "Yeah. Bit of a headache is all. Well, that, and a whole lot of mad at Eggman!"

Shadow smiled. Sonic smiled, too.

"Tails, Knuckles, and Amy can finish this up," Sonic said. "Let's go destroy Eggman's mind-control machine."

Sonic was about to speed to the villain's hideout when he noticed Shadow wasn't joining him.

"Hey, I was just here to help you get free. Now that that's done—good job freeing yourself, by the way—I'm out," Shadow said.

"Shadow, if Eggman did it to me, he can do it to you, too," Sonic said.

Shadow opened his mouth to say something, but quickly closed it. He realized Sonic was right. "Let's destroy that machine!" Shadow said.

Sonic and Shadow raced at full speed to Eggman's hideout.

〉〉〉〉〉〉〉〉

Eggman didn't realize Sonic had been freed from the mind-control device. If he had, maybe he could've prepared his defenses for Sonic and Shadow's arrival. The two hedgehogs burst into Eggman's lab and in a blur dismantled the mind-control device right before Eggman's eyes. Eggman barely had time to say anything before the machine was completely destroyed.

"My perfect creation!" Eggman yelled, falling to the floor with the millions of pieces of his sound-wave machine. "I'll get you for this! Both of you!"

"You'll have to catch us first," Sonic said with a sneer.

Sonic and Shadow ran out of the lair side by side.

"So, think you can keep up?" Sonic said.

"Do you?" Shadow asked.

The rivals picked up speed. The race was on. The blue

and black blurs sped away, moving toward the horizon at an immeasurable pace. Sonic was free from Eggman's grasp and deep down was grateful for Shadow's help.

But he'd never let him know that.

DOPPELGÄNGER

Tails was working in the lab, assisted by Amy Rose and Knuckles, building a massive vehicle. No one really knew exactly what it would do, but Tails was just happy to be working together with his friends. He often did this—started building something without knowing what it would become. It made him feel like an artist. As Amy Rose handed him a wrench and he tightened a bolt joining two large pieces of metal together, Tails smiled, knowing something awesome would be the end result.

"Do you know what this is going to be yet, Tails?" Amy Rose asked.

"Whatever it is, it'll probably break down on its first use," Knuckles joked.

Tails smiled, and said, "Not yet. It's a type of ground vehicle; sort of like a solar-powered tank, but faster. I want to add massive tank-like treads to the bottom for sure."

From behind them, Sonic said, "That sounds amazing!" They all turned to face their friend, shocked by what they saw.

"S-Sonic?" Amy Rose asked.

The hedgehog entering the lab looked like Sonic, but older. His blue fur was tinted with grey, and his face seemed a little worn.

"Who are you?" Knuckles asked, tensing.

"Relax, Knuckles. I'm Sonic. I'm just Sonic from the future," Future Sonic said.

Tails wasn't convinced. "Time travel's impossible. How'd you get here?"

Future Sonic strode around the room, in awe of the tech filling Tails' lab, and seemingly ignoring the question.

"Can you believe we used all this stuff? Talk about the dark ages!" Future Sonic said.

Just then, Sonic—the real Sonic—entered the lab and stopped cold in his tracks.

"Who are you?" Sonic asked Future Sonic.

Future Sonic sped next to Sonic. "I'm you. Or us. Or something. I'm from the future, anyway. Tails built a time machine, and I traveled back in time today!"

Sonic was annoyed and suspicious. First of all, he didn't like having a look-alike hanging around. And second, there's no way this guy could be him from the future.

"I built a time machine?" Tails whispered to himself, impressed.

"Why today?" Sonic asked.

Future Sonic continued exploring the lab, staring at the many inventions and almost-inventions that cluttered the space.

"Because two days from now, Team Sonic defeats Dr. Eggman once and for all! It's the most glorious victory in the history of all victories. And believe me, I know. Because I'm from the future!" Future Sonic said.

This piqued everyone's interest. Everyone, that is, except the real Sonic. Tails, Knuckles, and Amy Rose gathered around Future Sonic. Sonic stood off to the side, watching his friends grow more and more interested in the impostor.

"Greatest victory, huh? How'd we do that?" Knuckles asked.

"Oh, I can't tell you that, Knuckles," Future Sonic said. "But I'll help you guys prepare over the next couple of days."

"I can't get over the fact that I built . . . or am building . . . a time machine! How does it work? When do I build it?" Tails asked excitedly.

"Ummmm, Sonic, what happens to me—to us—in the future?" Amy Rose asked.

"Guys, guys, guys, I can't tell you any of that. You know, space-time continuum stuff. I don't want the universe to implode by screwing up the time line!" Future Sonic said.

Future Sonic led the group out of the lab, passing in front of Sonic who was leaning against a far wall. Future Sonic shot Sonic a look that seemed to say, "I'm taking over." Sonic felt anger rising within him. He felt replaced. He was mad at his friends for believing so easily. They'd betrayed him. Something was up. This guy was an impostor, Sonic was absolutely sure of that. But how was he going to prove it?

Future Sonic and the gang were gathered around the table eating lunch. Future Sonic was impressing everyone with stories from the future. Amy Rose, Tails, and Knuckles were soaking in everything Future Sonic was telling them.

"No, really! The cars fly!" Future Sonic said.

"But how do they maintain sufficient speed to stay in the air but not so fast to cause lots of accidents and injuries?" Tails asked.

Future Sonic shrugged. "I for sure don't know that. What do I look like? Some kind of brainiac like you, Tails? They just fly."

Sonic burst into the room and got in Future Sonic's face.

"I don't know who you are, but I don't believe for one minute you're me from the future," Sonic said with a snarl.

Future Sonic laughed and pushed Sonic away from him. "I forgot how grumpy I used to be!" he said.

Sonic didn't let up. He came nose to nose with Future Sonic. "All right, buster. If you're really me, prove it. I'm the fastest being in the universe. You should be just as fast as me. Let's go."

Future Sonic glanced around the table, a little nervous. "C'mon, let's not get crazy here, Sonic. I mean, I'm a lot older than you. I don't know if—"

Sonic slapped the table. "Aha! I knew you were a liar! You know you can't keep up with me. See guys! He's not me. He won't even race me."

Future Sonic stood up quickly from the table.

"If you'd let me finish, I was going to say I'm a lot older than you. I don't know if you can keep up with me. I'm just as fast as you; maybe faster."

Sonic grew hot. He couldn't believe the audacity of this faker. "It's on. Right now."

Moments later, the group was outside. Sonic and Future Sonic were side by side behind a line drawn in the dirt. No one noticed as Future Sonic slipped a small chip onto Sonic's shoe.

"On your marks. Get set," Tails called, raising a siren blaster in the air. "GO!"

The siren blared, and the two Sonics were off. Their course would take them over the nearby hills, to the beach, through the city, and back to the starting line in one giant circle. They were neck and neck as the race began.

"Faster, huh?" Sonic sneered at Future Sonic next to him.

"Just watch," Future Sonic said.

Future Sonic flipped a switch on his wristband and starting going faster, and then faster—and faster still. Within seconds, Future Sonic was blazing ahead of Sonic in a blue-grey blur. Sonic skidded to a stop, shocked, and watched Future Sonic run out of sight. *This is impossible. Simply impossible,* he thought.

Back at the starting line, Future Sonic returned about fifteen seconds after leaving. Everyone was shocked that he completed the course that quickly. Even more surprising was that it took Sonic a full two minutes more to complete the course and return to the starting line.

"How . . . did . . . how did you . . . how did you do that so fast?" Sonic said as he gasped for breath.

"You know, more experience," Future Sonic said, kicking the toe of Sonic's shoe. "Now, can we start prepping for the big, final battle against Dr. Eggman?"

Knuckles and Tails excitedly walked with Future Sonic back toward the lab. Future Sonic looked over his shoulder back at Sonic and winked. Amy Rose put her arm around Sonic.

"Are you okay? I've never seen you so winded," she said.

Sonic brushed her arm off and stood up straight,

squinting suspiciously at Future Sonic.

"This isn't right, Amy. I don't know what it is, but something's up with that guy. I had to push myself the most I ever had, and he still beat me by a lot."

"Sonic, just because he's faster than you doesn't mean anything. He's from the future. He's got better shoes, better training, and more experience," Amy Rose said, hoping her words would bring some comfort to her friend.

Sonic shook his head. "No, Amy. That's not it. It's not just the running. It's something else. And I'm going to find out."

"I'm sure it's nothing," Amy Rose said and jogged to catch up with her friends.

As Sonic watched his friends leave, he felt something strange in his shoes. His feet started moving. Before he knew it, Sonic was running—running away from the lab. And he couldn't stop. His shoes were forcing him.

Somehow, Sonic knew, he had to get his shoes off and get back to his friends before it was too late.

》》》》》》》

Future Sonic, Knuckles, Amy Rose, and Tails returned to the lab and continued working on the tank. They were making good progress. Tails thought it would be up and running by the end of the day.

"So, you need to show me how this thing works," Future Sonic said.

Tails looked confused. "I thought you knew already. Don't you lead us into battle in it?"

Future Sonic paused, gathering his thoughts, "Um . . . well . . . it was a long time ago. Tech has advanced way beyond that. I need a refresher on remedial tech like this."

"Uh . . . okay . . . ," Tails said.

Tails gave Future Sonic an overview of the controls, teaching him how to drive the tank and fire its laser cannon.

"This is so cool," Future Sonic said.

A short time later, the trio tightened the final bolts. The treads were attached, and the tank was finished. Tails stepped back to admire his work.

"I gotta admit, you did a good job with this, Tails," Knuckles said.

"It's perfect for the final battle against Dr. Eggman tomorrow," Future Sonic said. "Remember! We move at dawn!"

Knuckles turned to Tails. "I'm out. Gotta prepare for tomorrow's battle. Call me if you need me," Knuckles said as he walked out the door.

"I better go, too," Amy Rose said. "I'm going to find Sonic. He was still pretty upset at the end of the race."

"That's because I beat him so badly," Future Sonic said as a

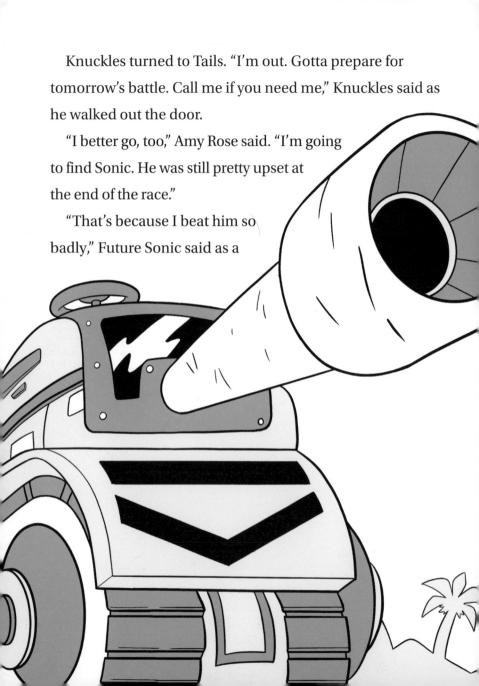

light on his wrist lit up and a strange beeping noise sounded. "I've, uh, gotta take this. Future communicator."

Future Sonic disappeared into a back room.

>>>>>>>>>

Future Sonic tapped the blinking light on his wrist. A holographic image of Dr. Eggman shot upward.

"Everything is going according to plan. I have access to the weapon," Future Sonic said.

"Good. Good," Dr. Eggman said. "They believe you? That you're from the future?"

"Yes."

"You planted the permanent running chip on Sonic's shoes?" Eggman asked.

"Yes."

"You are my greatest creation! A robot so lifelike that even Sonic's closest friends don't realize you're a robot. I'm a genius!" Eggman roared in celebration.

"The attack begins at dawn," Future Sonic said, pushing

the light on his wrist and closing the holographic image.

He turned to leave the room, but stopped dead in his tracks. Tails was standing in the doorway, eyes wide, mortified.

"T-Tails. How long have you been standing there?" Future Sonic asked.

"Sonic was right! You are a fake!" Tails said.

Future Sonic lifted his right arm and blasted ropes at Tails. The ropes wrapped their way around Tails from head to toe before he even had a chance to escape. Future Sonic grabbed the cocooned fox and dragged him to the closet.

"Sorry to have to do this to you, Tails, but I can't have you stopping our attack tomorrow," Future Sonic said. "Actually, I'm not sorry."

Future Sonic slammed the closet door shut.

》》》》》》》

It took what felt like hours, but the speed chip overloaded and freed Sonic from its trap. He returned to Tails' lab, but it appeared abandoned. It made sense, though. It was the middle of the night. Almost dawn, actually. Sonic moved to leave when he heard what sounded like a muffled cry for help coming from a back room.

Sonic found the source of the noise. It was coming from inside a closet, which the hedgehog opened. Sonic leaped back in shock, seeing Tails tied up. He quickly removed Tails' bonds.

"You were right, Sonic!" Tails gasped. "That Future Sonic isn't from the future at all. He's an advanced robot created by Eggman!"

Sonic gritted his teeth.

"There's more. He put some kind of chip on your shoes so you'd have to run forever," Tails said.

"I know. When he kicked my foot, it set off the chip," Sonic said. "But it's not a problem anymore."

Tails moved into the lab.

"Oh no," Tails said. "The tank is gone, and it's almost dawn."

Knuckles and Amy Rose arrived to join what they thought was going to be the climactic battle with Dr. Eggman. Tails and Sonic quickly brought them up to speed.

"We've got to stop him before he uses the tank," Sonic said to his team.

"How could I have been so stupid? I taught him how to use the tank!" Tails said.

Sonic shook his head. "No time for that now, Tails. We've got to find him and stop him."

Outside the lab, the tank's treads had left a trail in the ground, which led to the outskirts of town.

"If he's planning to use that on the town—" Amy Rose began.

"I'm gonna get that guy!" Knuckles said, slamming his fist into his other hand.

The sun was starting to peek out over the horizon.

"There's no time, Knuckles. I've got to do this one by myself." And without another word, Sonic shot off in a streak, following the tread prints.

>>>>>>>>

Impostor Sonic plowed over the rolling hills and fields that separated Tails' lab from the nearby town. Dr. Eggman had programmed him to gain Team Sonic's trust, steal some kind of weapon, and use that weapon to scare the townspeople into abandoning the town, leaving it for Eggman to come in and conquer. It was all going according to plan.

Fake Sonic saw a blip on his external sensor. Something was coming up on him from behind—and coming fast. *Sonic!* The robot turned the tank's laser cannon around and started blasting lasers at Sonic.

Sonic dodged the laser blasts. Within seconds, he jumped on top of the tank. He opened the hatch and dropped into the command seat next to Fake Sonic. The two wrestled each other, trying to gain control of the tank. The laser cannon's turret spun wildly, shooting laser blasts indiscriminately.

"You can't stop me. I'm a better version of you," Impostor Sonic yelled.

"No. You're. Not!" Sonic screamed, grabbing the robot's arms.

Sonic threw the robot out of the tank's controls and

on top of the tank. The tank continued to roll toward the town as Sonic and his doppelgänger again wrestled one another. Fake Sonic pinned Sonic to the roof of the tank.

"Face it. I'm better than you. You'll never defeat me!" he said.

Sonic brought a foot up to the robot's chest. "I've had enough of you! Real will always be better than robots! Always!"

Sonic kicked out, sending the robot backward. Fake Sonic came back toward Sonic, planning to throw him off the tank. As he got close, though, the robot tripped over a large bolt on top of the tank. He slipped off, landing on the ground in front of it. The massive treads slowly rolled over him, crushing the metal monster.

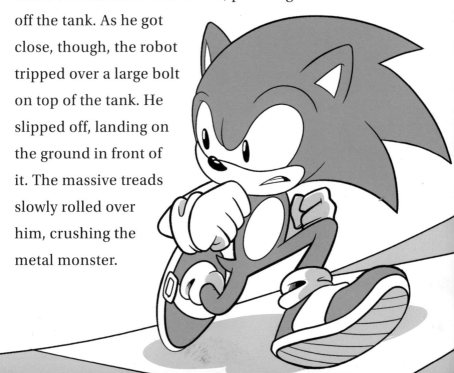

Sonic slipped back into the tank, shutting it down. It was over.

〉〉〉〉〉〉〉〉

Later, Sonic rejoined his friends at Tails' lab. Tails and Knuckles were dismantling the tank. Now that Eggman knew about it, Tails didn't want their enemy to steal it again.

Amy Rose looked sad. "I'm sorry I doubted you, Sonic."

"Hey, no big deal. I got to whip his butt and save the day," Sonic said. "Best part is, we still get to make our own future!"